LIVING AT THE EDGE

Short stories by Ian Stephen

with illustrations and cover-design by Malcolm Maclean

Printed by Aberdeen People's Press
163 King Street Aberdeen.

ISBN 0 946210 01 2 (Limp edition)
ISBN 0 946210 00 4 (Hardback)

m_b Machair Books, Stornoway and Aberdeen.

Copies available post free from:
3 Killegray Court, Stornoway, Isle of Lewis.

Contents

Acknowledgements

Grateful thanks to the following where some of these stories have been published or broadcast:

EILEEN AN FHRAOICH; 2nd EDITION; NEW EDINBURGH REVIEW; NORTHERN LIGHT; NORTHSOUND; RADIO SCOTLAND; STAND; THE GREEN DOOR (Belgium)

Four of them are also included on the cassette tape: FATHOMS AND METRES which is available from Croft Recordings, Tong Studio, Isle of Lewis.

Thanks to Graeme Roberts of Aberdeen University for his criticism and encouragement and to Robin Callander for his advice on publishing and marketing.

'Living At The Edge' is indebted to many storytellers, too numerous to mention by name, but particular thanks to Audy MacIver, Kenny (Safety) Smith and Calum Grant.

This book could not have been published without the aid of The Scottish Arts Council.

1. **TRAVELLERS**
    FIndlay and Willack and Lisach
    Willack and Lisach
    Householding
    On the Bones

FINDLAY AND WILLACK AND LISACH

Findlay's motives had nothing to do with the daughter, he knew himself that much anyway, so he said, and no it was no desire to exalt his spirit onto a pedestal that prompted him up to the roof of Willack's house. The roof had to be tarred. That was a mucky job, fair enough, but one for Findlay to take relish in, as he told me himself. Especially during that period of his existence and that wasn't so long ago either.

Not long, I remember too, since Findlay emerged from out his own hut. It was on a lonlier moor, but only an hour or two from Willack's more permanent camp. Findlay came out from under the shadow of the weighty tomes of 'modern masters', not that there is anything wrong with these thinkers but total immersion in any ideas is near enough drowning. Anyway the volumes had always seemed incongruous there on his improvised shelves, up from the diminishing sacks of animal meal. Yes and above the coffee-jars full of Findlay's own personal supplies. The stock of rice and pulses stayed fairly constant there. It was not so much that he was set on starving himself but, in his own words, if there was bread around there was not much impulse to make up his own fodder.

He had the donkey for company then. The beast had a biblical aura when seen from a few yards' distance but if you got close to it and left your own blinkers behind you could see even then it was a bit impractical. The creature looked fine though when it followed behind the hand that fed it, out for a walk, across the few miles to Willack's.

This tarry-roofed structure was a hundred or two paces from a new bungalow with walls and green railings around it, a second house the man had built before he was quite old. Money for it had come from scrap, - metal and wood and all the other stuff that people called rubbish. Willack and the strong daughter habited the thing for nearly a year before returning to the original structure with the one stone gable and the stove and the stout frame that was all coated with a bitumastic smell.

So, young Findlay with his Testamental beard arrived to step out from himself into that shelter and even, on that day he spoke of, up onto the roof.

He was splendid he said, in the borrowed shirt, striped in wooly cotton, going to his knees and absorbing more of the tar himself, becoming more of a sight that day as the hour went on - a thing from a ballad or a bawdy song. Willack watched, stroked his moustache and handed up the materials.

Findlay remembered coming down hungry and just as well. The daughter Lisach, had taken care over the dinner. She could stand back a bit now, no physical weight behind her, but confident. The hair was loosely tied back, no grey in it and the auburn light in the strands that came over her forehead.

Findlay was ready and willing to take all the food that was on offer but when the old man used the word 'payment' the young one was ready to get stroppy. Till Willack explained himself with a bit more care.

The mention was of them both knowing what it was like to be out a few steps away from everyone else. But at least Willack had his daughter and his own son was not so far away now in that Bungalow along with his wife and bairns. Glad they all were of that too, family as neighbours, though the odd shout would out itself, though you couldn't worry too much about that. But what he was saying, Willack to Findlay, quietly, while Lisach was busy, was that, the rest of the family being so near, he could spare the girl. Not for ever or anything like it, but a week or two anyway to see how they got on.

Since his son's wife could do all the cooking. Mind you he would miss Lisach in the evenings. She was getting the way of that melodeon now too. Aye and Findlay would need the warmth even more than the food, since that new stove of his was no damn use, whatever the plans and designs he'd built it from though the work in it was something you had to admire. Anyway, as to the matter in hand, she was a strong girl and the good ten years she had over him was all the better since Findlay needed an even firmer hand than that brown donkey.

But Lisach had the bowls out now and was turned to the men, so her father changed his tone to inform Findlay the beard was too long and a moustache was a better idea altogether.

The way Findlay reflected all this to me, he was more gladdened than embarrassed or anything else. This was no light talk. It was the highest honour, though of course he could never accept. Nearer twice-ten years the daughter had over him but that was nothing in itself. She had the firmest cheeks, a fine tough beauty but the girl had a life and a mind of her own, willing or no to go back over the moor for a while.

Yet Findlay must have given the offer more serious thought than he let-on. It would be nearer months than a year, after the tarring of the roof, that he shifted from his own hut, with the winter starting, and took a bed in our house, his cousins at the edge of town. I had the other bed in our big room and near enough to Findlay's to hear him speaking from his state of half-sleep. I listened to him well, late the same night he'd been so consciously telling me of huts and daughters, security, reward and principles.

He rose up, head, shoulders and pelvis from his sleep and said it out loud - older yes, she was, but he could do worse than marriage. There was love there, he said and sank down again but only for seconds before his head bobbed up to say no, no, maybe it was tiredness.

There is no way of knowing if Findlay will stay with us here until the spring or if he will always feel the need to go out that bit, further from the town. Certainly he is showing no signs of looking for a mate, unless he is silent and dark about it. I cannot judge the man's capacity for darkness but he is certainly incapable of sustained silence.

But, as he put it himself, he could have done worse than Lisach. Her and the old man brought the warmth to him though it was alway Findlay who made the move across the moor. Maybe the problem was that he wanted to marry the old man as well as the daughter. He wanted all the love and all the yarns he could get - and there's none of us so different.

WILLACK AND LISACH

She offered me soup and held the loaf out to me often enough but it was only the once I laid down the fish on her table.

It was a mighty pot she used too but it had to serve them every day, her and the old man. Soup was no starter: it made their meal and, no mistake, there was little ritual in the breaking of the bread.

She knew the money was well spent on the local loaf. The stuff had more substance. She put the knife rather than the poetic hand to the splitting of the crust. Bread went further that way, but she measured the slice to match your leaness. I always got offered a doorstep.

Lisach would not have weighed me up that way if she'd seen the Sunday dinner I'd shifted. Whenever I did make it to their place it was always after a hefty indulgence. Bloated or no, I should never have refused a thing that was held out to me there. I could bite my lip at that now.

The old man was happy if the offer was made but Lisach went further. She wanted to see you eat. She would be the youngest daughter but had double my years, - yes and has them still. And she had - yes and has - one of those faces that are strong looking at twenty but as fine at forty.

If Lisach had been in another setting you'd say she she was good at the entertaining. She missed not a word or a look of the eye but her knife was never still. Carrots and cabbage in the pot in order. She couldn't have anything going mushy.

At the onions she was an artist, chopping them first one way then with a single flick to the other. Cleanly. From the board to the hand and in the pot, all in one movement.

That grace in Lisach must have been present every time I was in that house. It was wasted on me when I would sit under the old man's moustache and take in his tobacco-cloud. Willack had an artistry of his own that came out in his breathing a glow to his boyish days, even behind the criss-cross of cold feet and sad ponies; biting harness. Yes and people who would accept him in for tea, make the offer, and them living right next door to others who said Tinker as if it was a spit.

I sat on the stool. All Willack said was from the big

chair under the photograph. What a frame that picture had - it must have been salvaged from the remains of an Old Master. The Willack in it was too young for more than a hint of a moustache, but was kilted and buckled.

They'd been pleased to accept the travellers then and there, in the army. There was no malice in most of the lads. You had your leg pulled like anyone else.

But he told me I was lucky not to have been around then and I wasn't to listen to them who said it brought people together. So it did - the ones left. The Germans too. It must have done the same to them.

Lisach would not intrude on her father's stories but she would have taken her onion knife to me rather than let me go from their place without taking tea. I'd always drink it to the last drop and was careful not to grimace at the sugary bit towards the bottom. I couldn't tell Lisach I didn't indulge in the white crystals. Tea had sugar and soup had onions. She saw it like that and she wasn't far wrong. What's the difference? Sugar in the tea or in my daily weakness for a fancy biscuit.

But it took a while to see what was in that woman, yes and still is. And the last few times I was in that house the focus was all on Lisach. The old man's lungs were going and his voice with them. Lisach could speak out.

My sister, was she still at the nursing? And that friend I'd brought from the other island, Shetland wasn't it? He was still trying to be a teacher? Wasn't Africa terrible, beyond everything but... Every people had their troubles but the black man had always got the worst of it.

But her father himself, she wouldn't hide it from me, he wasn't well. It was breaking him, not having his voice. He still liked it if there was life about the place. People speaking away. He didn't miss much. Was I still working out there, the estate, still with the ponies?

Yes and now I gave them apple-cores, to bribe them, not sugar. That's what he told me once himself.

I glanced over and his nod came now to shock me. I'd been talking about him as if he was gone. My chair twisted round right then, so I could see both faces, Lisach's and her father's.

'Boot and saddle' they called me out there. I'd be rubbing in oil to the straps so they wouldn't chafe, while my dinner was getting cold. Maybe your father would say I was getting too soft... But what? Were they feeding me all right? Fat of the land. And no, I wasn't letting anyone order me about.

She didn't like mentioning it, but if I could get hold of a decent bit of fish. It was all he would eat.

Lisach nodded over then to the pot on the stove. He wouldn't even take that. Lisach and I had a full bowl each.

When next I was there I jumped from the Land-Rover but kept its engine running. I wouldn't keep the boys long.

Lisach did smile but it was a strange one as the fish, two sea-trout, came down on the table.

Her brother, the eldest one that was married but lived not so far away, was sitting in with her. He said they were beauties all right.

She just rose from her chair and steered me in next door. It must have been her own room. The old man's bed was always in the first room where the stove was.

He lay in here now. She saw my shock and spoke to calm me. Didn't he look beautiful. She made me touch him. The moustache was all combed and spreading right out.

He looks beautiful, I said.

HOUSEHOLDING

S uch a menage a deux could only ever have a very limited duration. This is not because one is brown and the other white: one more verbose, the other more blunt. It was an arrangement held together by something more necessary than convenience but there was and is no sexual aspect to their relationship.

The two men were not all that odd together, except that one worked in silk shirts and ties, the other in dungarees and whatever had been near at hand in the morning.

In fact there was a measure of trade. The occasional fine, pale shirt began to appear from out the armpits or at the neck of the denin overalls. On certain days some cologne after-shave was detectable in the labourer's beard. The brown-skinned, clean-shaven man did not object to the seizure. Cooking occurred on a special occasion and the white-skinned, bearded man was an artist in his own primitive way.

In exchange for the long-term borrowing of garments and perfumes he had nothing to offer but that practical art. His one sheep could not be counted in the bargain. It was lodged in a neighbour's deep-freeze and exactly counterbalanced the other man's sack of A.1. Basmati rice. But the performance of preparing food appeased any controversies over fair shares of borrowing. For this, the cook rose at six-thirty in the morning, perhaps catching in the first and last quiet of the day, the murmered breath of dawn-prayers from the next room.

The quality of exertion involved in making a decent meal was not worth it for two. The cook responded well to a threat of great numbers. He wore plimsoles at the feet of his dungarees and no shirt. In return, the marchandiser abandoned his father's shop for the morning and went in quest of mushrooms and aubergines. Meat would have been demanded from the freeze the night before and the neighbour warned and invited.

I found myself at the last big dinner. The lease required... Even if that lease had stayed static, these two were individuals. It had been a successful short-term arrangement but they both had their needs. A finale was in order. The elderly neighbour was compassionate. She did not object to the rock-band since the boys had nowhere else to play, but the noise had to be over at 10.30. Yes, she might come along as well, for a while at least, before the music came, anyway.

My presence was required. Not simply because I was a fellow labourer with one of the pair and so was slightly acquainted with the daily runnings of the house-hold, since I had to pick up my workmate in the morning and return him in the evening. The role of fiddler was the relevant one, even though I admitted a rusty bow. Who else was coming? A rock-band and friends. Nobody likes to appear prejudiced but did they really think the two styles of music would go? No. No. Yes. Yes. I saw. They hoped to build up a fire for a post 10.30 second phase to follow the new-wave music. Fine.

The room was not yet shaking. There was plenty of space since most of the removal had already been accomplished. The neighbour sat in the only surviving armchair and was being well-plied with young company, tea and the shortbread she had herself brought. No. She really did quite like curry but it didn't like her. But thanks. And yes, she could go another cup.

She was finding it easier than me to accept the figures in cropped hair and strange ornamentation. She had, after all, the advantage of having lived through my own age-group's period of long, more freely-falling hair, and more delicate pendants and clothes. Cotton, rather than leather had been our style. Floating rather than tight. But she really had to be going now and mind - 10.30. Fair was fair.

She went and the room started to shake. The fiddle lay like a timid dog to the side of the armchair I had taken over. Yes, but later. And yes, I would eat something later.

It was a new style of moving to me but the brown skinned friend set an example in adaptability. And my unlikely looking workmate with a best shirt under clean dungarees. He had abandoned even the plimsoles for ease of movement. Someone pulled me up from the chair to tentative steps. She had a pale blue feather somehow fixed to her ear. All jumped and somehow came together. We took turns at looking intense and grinning. Miraculously the loudspeakers and amplifiers ceased to vibrate at 10.30. I was quite sorry and not only because the fiddle had to somehow follow that.

Food helped. And fire. Two plain chairs, 'not worth removing' were sacrificed. They probably had woodworm anyhow, someone said in justification. The resultant blaze was stimulating, but tamed within the grate. Wood was added, only as required. Two very large pans, already heated, appeared from the kitchen along with many small bowls and one washing-up basin, clean and brimful of salad. An error of judgement had sent the cutlery away too soon but we all had fingers and all the time in the world, or at least the remaining night and day before the lease was over.

Piquancy of spiced mutton was offset by rice, cooked simply, with restraint. Greenstuff and crisp, sliced raw onions freshened everything. We were perhaps fifteen, perhaps twenty and we were all within sight of the fire. No-one was in the armchair.

Until the father of my workmate appeared. He had come for a quiet word and could not hide it, he was a little taken aback. He was given the seat. Would he have something to eat? No. Sure? It was his own son who had cooked it, with a little technical advice on spice mixtures.

Well... but yes, it had been a long time since he'd taken his meal. Mutton, yes, local stuff. Their own. Spices? No, he wasn't bothered by that. He'd had his curries in the army. These purple vegetables in it? Yes he'd seen them before.

And the Moslem lad who shared the house with his son spooned out food and told a story about aubergines. His own father - and he too would be here if he had not been embarrassed over the meal... there were customs which were a necessity to some and it was better to stay away than refuse food. But yes, his own father said that a man should choose his wife by how well and how often she cooked aubergines. Perhaps turnips would be the equivalent in this country, being, like aubergines in the East, cheap and plentiful.

If you were interested in a girl you should arrange to be invited to her parents' house at least twice in succession, when she was cooking. You should say on the first night, this food is delicious, what is it? She would reply, aubergines, or rather turnips. On the second night you should be able to say again that the food tasted different and if again she had made use of turnips, you should try to marry her. She would be blessed with creativity but also an economic mind.

The labourer's father, who was present in the armchair, laid his hand on the fiddle. Who could play? So I did what I could and trusted that any snatched or jerked movements of the bow on the strings would not break the prevailing intimacy. Many heads, mostly with short, hackled hair and among them the girl with the blue feather, were now more still and listening. We had danced the discords out of our system for the time being. I found myself remembering a quotation: 'For everything there is a season...'

It was months rather than weeks when the two ex-householders and myself again met. I had by then lost my work-mate to his individual way, living twenty miles, distant, on a one-man job. Neither had his friend and I seem much of each other but the Moslem lad eventually appeared. It was late at night. He informed me it was my services as a driver which were required this time. The fiddle could stay at home. I would have to be ready to wake at 6 am. If I was able to help out, that was.

I pulled the cushions off the settee for him to sleep on. He woke me with the sound of early prayers.

My guest had already obtained the two bags of animal-feeding concentrates which were needed by his now-distant friend. The telephone was a great device. All was ready in his father's car, specially borrowed, but he had not passed his test and... I could co-drive. We all had to be at work in some very few hours. My boss would be even less understanding than his father.

Some little snow was on the twenty miles of road. More on the fields and a great deal on the higher land outside the fences. That was why the sheep needed special food. I knew how our bearded friend needed his sheep. Few men can completely satisfy their being with their daily work. I have my music. One friend has his animals. The other friend has the persuasive eloquence which convinced me that this pre-dawn excursion was a sensible one.

It was not a reconciliation because there had been no quarrel. Only the inevitabilities of terms of lease: and virtuoso personalities.

The one whose name I cannot even pronounce had brought his bottle of French after-shave as well as the sheep-feed. My ex-workmate rubbed it vigorously into his hair and beard, the perfume that was, not the concentrates, and shouted the offer of tea as he did so. No time - we had to drive back to work.

The one who kept sheep ran back into the small house and returned brandishing something in the air. It was a stiff leg of meat. No, he did not intend to cudgel us for refusing his offer. Salt-mutton, he said. No, we were not getting it to take away. We had to return and eat it here, with him on his own ground. It did not matter when. It would keep.

ON THE BONES

A few times, he said, he was on the bare bones of his backside. He did not mean, he said, getting by on bread and marg, so much as not really getting by at all.

1.

London was the scene of his first experience of stomach-pangs. It was a long way from the security of the three meat meals a day he had been raised on. Being cold at night was part of the hunger. And after the summer, being cold most of the time.

Except one weekend when a few of them made it to one of those seaside towns, pier and all, but deserted of course. There was plenty of driftwood on the beach. It all got left there in the winter. Until their happy bunch of very lightly seasoned

Londoners came along. No-one bothered them. Their fires were always burning. Tin-cans were boiling with winkles. All the people sleeping out there had got at least a twinge of gut-ache but all had lived to sing out loud - and return to the city.

London seemed both worse and fresher after. You got by. There were always things to break up the time: like three weekly events that he could remember.

The weekly scrub took place in Harrods of Knightsbridge. They were reliable for all the hot water you could use and everyone that came in to the Gentlemen's room was too polite to complain or even comment on the bare-backed two-or-three-some who scrubbed each other by brimming and steaming sinks.

The warm sleep of the week was when their band boarded a train that had come from quite far North and arrived at too early an hour to loose its passengers on the cold city streets. So the travellers who had come all the way would doze in the radiatored carriages and wake to find more of the seats occupied than they remembered.

From 5.15 to 7.30 of a Sunday morning it was blissful for the invaders of the train. And the big feed of the week was to follow right on. Those hungry ones had to walk a little further than the restaurant carriage for it, though.

One of their former number had landed a job in a

small but select hotel. Sunday breakfast was there a fine and traditional meal for the very few who chose to observe the ritual. Most of the guests preferred to bide their time and make a dinner of the lunch.

So the hand-over point for what they failed to do justice to, was the telephone-box across the road. The kitchen door would be flung open and a young man with blue-spotted trousers and a very fine neckerchief would sprint over with the cardboard box and be slapped on the back by the agent for the hungry who took charge of the goods and conveyed the lot to the waiting dozen. They would walk on and pass that box around like a big bag of crisps. Kippers would come out and kidneys and bacon: fried eggs for colour-contrast and here and there a fig for sweetness.

'What, no corn-flakes!' someone would say, and another: 'He might at least have thrown in some pineapple-juice.'

2.

He was out of London when he next hit stoney ground, but it was hardly barren country. Oxford area: rivers and all. He was alone in it this time. Fine trees, but nothing you could eat growing on them. Not in the spring anyway.

He was hopeful though, when he remembered that a newly married cousin had gone to make her home somewhere in this very area. He even remembered her husband's name. Right. Phone-box. Phonebook. Address. Amazing. No need even to pick up the phone. Anyway he could not afford to fiddle about with coins.

So he went directly to the relevant Oxford suburb. His cousin was in. She was quite surprised, really pleased to see him and was quite taken with his skull-cap. She knew he had come from a different world. She knew he needed food and did not get flustered but told him some of her neighbours and acquaintances were coming round for a sherry and he could have first go at the sandwiches and he was welcome anyway and he would have his dinner with them when her man came back from work.

There was no flag in the conversation even when the hens came for their party: well-groomed hens but they were quite relaxed about the man in their midst. He was interesting after all: an artistic appearance.

That cousin, the darling, saw him fed in the afternoon and at dinner and at breakfast. No show about it. And the husband's breed of humour was just about palatable.

3.
His third story of hunger was, he admitted, more of a laugh than a lust after the necessities. It could only happen in the country cottage scene. He was more content out there than he'd ever been but though he never saw himself as isolated, he had to get used to planning out things. Like with food and with seeing people. It all took a bit of balancing out.

He got himself stuck one weekend. Hadn't met a soul for the seven-day stretch. Missed the baker's van. Hadn't got a store-cupboard organised. Lost the last of the tatties in the fire he'd tried to bake them in. Yes he was hungry. At least he had warmth.

It was the cat helped him get some food and some activity on the go. He stole two sparrows from her, or blackbirds or something. They took a lot of plucking.

A friend came by when the pot was simmering. She'd brought a round of scone. She would have been welcome anyway, even empty-handed, but this was something else. He said she'd timed it well. Dinner was ready.

She asked what it was and he said meat and she said she was glad he'd used up all the bitter brown lentils.

They sat to it. What little meat there was made a good gravy to go with the round of bread. She said it was good and asked what kind of meat it was and he said nightingales or something - he didn't know for sure. He was not much up on bird-life.

She said he was joking and he said he wasn't and she believed him and asked him how he'd got hold of them.

He pointed to the cheated cat and his guest did not know whether to laugh or not. Then she said she'd heard of song-birds as a French delicacy, but she

was sure the restauranters there didn't steal them
from the cats.

2. **YOUNG AND GETTING ON**
    Jimmy-Dan
    The Functional Bicycle
    Duncan
    Jubilee
    In the Wake

JIMMY-DAN

They say travelling lets you think. Whether or not this is true something was disturbing me, even on the city-bus, all the way up the long avenue as the branches were brushing the top deck.

The awkward bundle of fruit had something to do with it. It was easier to make the visit carrying a token of something or other in a chain-store polythene bag. There had been too much bother about choice of grapes, bananas and pears, all really of uniform quality, even under the harsh lighting of the downstairs food-section of a very large shop. These fruits might be easier on his stomach than citrus or chocolate or magazines. But I had spent too long within the walls of the inner town.

There was another avenue to go through, by foot this time, between the bus-stop and the high clock tower of a grey building. A notice-board, placed half way along the drive, stated visiting times, but I had telephoned before and claimed to be a friend from a distance away and could not manage it in the evening. A female voice had smiled over the lines and said of course they would make an exception. Even with that privilege taken for granted they would not take so well to visitors at meal times and hospital meals are always gotten through early and efficiently.

The sleet of March did not help, up the way to the door. Nor was the forced temperature of halls and corridors very encouraging. I was equally impotent over the level of thermometers and with a mood that was giving me self-conscious footsteps. A nurse helped. Or, judging by her uniform, she might have been a sister but despite her red epaulettes she brought me towards Jimmy-Dan. She steered a way through the swing doors into the ward.

'O yes,' she said. 'You must be the exception. You're from up North. Come right in. What? Fruit? Yes that would be alright for him. We've a few different kinds of stomach case in here you know. Here we are. Well at least this is his bed anyway.'

I stayed by it but she was saying that my friend wandered about quite a bit. She would see if he was down the ward at the television.

'Thanks.' But she had already set off to track him.

I noticed the bottles while waiting. Most bedside tables had an orange-juice and lemon-barley medley at the head of them. Fruit-juice might have been all right for Dan but I had a vague notion about acids affecting inflamed stomachs. His table was bare of any bottles. This might have been due to his internal condition or the absence could be simply because this specialised treatment could only be had three hundred miles from where his family had settled.

There was no fruit bowl either, only a little shiny dish that was placed so as to be convenient for him to vomit into.

Dan came up then, walking slowly, but looking as big as ever until he was breathing beside me and I could see it was thick pyjamas and the dressing gown that were padding him out. His hair was brushed back as usual. It was very thick for a man in his fifties but all in control. He was as neat as this even when he was in his boiler-suit. Strange that his face seemed smoother, at least under the rough area about his eyes. His grip was limp but he had never been one for trying to show his strength in an over-masculine handshake.

We both sank down to sit on the firmness of his bed.

'Thanks boy, thanks now - for coming up.'

I told him not to be daft. This should have been

earlier in the week and earlier in the day. My brother had sent me word.

Dan asked where exactly I was living now.

'Not so far out along the coast. Fifteen miles from here but I think when the nurses heard the accent they thought I'd come the full three hundred. Maybe that's why they let me in, out of hours.'

Did he know this town I'd shifted to?

Was I forgetting he took the truck all over the country to fill-up the load of scrap? But I wasn't doing that fifteen miles back and fore every day in to the college?

Yes to both and the travelling wasn't so bad. It beat getting the bus through the city. Then something else came to mind and I went ahead without thinking about whether it had the right tone for the situation. That was a good move.

'We had a bit of an accident last week,' I said and then had to explain it. 'Yes the bloddy wheel fell off.'

Dan gave his laugh but it hurt him.

'My mate took it well. We share the costs. It's an old Morris Traveller, he's got.'

'Like myself, falling to bits.' Dan said and my own smile was struggling.

'No, there's more than a thousand c.c.'s in you', I said but knew it was weak and then swore at him.

He took that better.

'But a wheel coming off. I've only seen that in the cartoons. How in Hell's name did you let a wheel fall off?'

I could only say it was sheer mechanical talent but my mate had said afterwards, a bit late in the day, that he thought he'd been hearing an extra rattle from somewhere.

'And you weren't bright enough, between the pair of you to get fixed up? Could you not have stolen one bolt from off all your other wheels and used them to fix the runaway back on?'

There was no answer to give and he did not look for one but our unease had nothing to do with our story. Neither of us could help being disturbed by the man in the next bed. The body was shifting and his face too. He could not ease over to change the way he was lying. A complex arrangement of tube-lines went from his arm, to surgical bottles fixed on a stand above his head.

'That old man there is having it bad,' Dan said it slow and quiet. 'He's like myself - can't hold any food down. That fellow there is stuck where he's put. He can't go up and down the place making a nuisance of himself. Pity. It would do him good. But Hell boy, I've got to say it - my own guts are bad the now - Hellish. They keep setting me a place at the table down there, three times a day but all I can hold on to is my cup of tea. Even soup - I tried it the day - but it ended up in that damned tin bowl there.

'Sure but I'm used to spewing up the guts now. I've been doing it for years. But what I says to all the doctors is that I couldn't care how often they've heard it before - it's being stuck in this one building that gets me. Sure, I says, I've got family ties and I see they're well done by. Even when I'm down here I phone them every night. Anyway, back there with them I'm still getting about a bit, in that old truck of ours, whatever my guts are like. And back home for supper and bed. Here boy, you know that yourself, you've been out in it with me.

'But I feel right stuck when I'm in here. So I says to the whole crowd of doctors, with all respects granted, what's the point of me being here? I've no faith in your tests, I says, as straight as that, but you're all tryers, I says; and none of you is giving up, but you've been sticking bits and pieces into my guts, I says, or else taking bits of me away, and you're still not agreeing on what's to be done. No but it's hard. They say they understand, right enough, about the walls, but what can they do? Like I say they're all workers in their way, you've got to give them that, but I grudge farting about here. I'm a bloody grafter myself boy, whatever else.'

I knew it, I told him and would never forget it, the day of the barrels. Copper, lead and the brass that nearly killed us - all stuff he'd boiled down into those oil-drums. Then I'd taken my tea and my couple of quid along with the rest of the squad. It was the toughest and best day's work of the lot.

'You'll be ashamed now, Dan, of my college-boy's hands,' I told him and showed the blisters from the weekend.

'A tattie-patch. A long one,' I proclaimed and admitted being soft, these days, for a job like that, but it was a good thing to tackle after a week in the books. Digging the length of this ward.

The last description hung heavy in the air but Dan had another go at smiling. His eyes were very nearly blue. I had never noticed that before. The colour was probably brought out against his paleness.

A girl in a blue overall went by us then, making her round. She handed out cups and asked the men who took their meals in bed if they wanted brown or white bread with their tea. I asked Dan if he would manage a bit of food with the others at the table up the ward.

'I might take a cup of tea with them in a while,' he said, 'but never mind about that, boy. Lean your head over, I've got a crack for you. We'll have to keep the clampers on the voice. We don't want to bother that old man there and anyway this damned voice of mine won't shout out the way I want it to.

'Anyway you're not going till I tell you about another doctor, a young fellow back home. This was before they thought of flying me down. Most of them in the practice were all right but this one had a hell of a smart bed-side voice, you know. And he says I was always phoning up and bothering him. If it wasn't for me it was for my kids. He called me Mister too and that made it worse. I says to him, quite gentle-like, it's like this doctor, I says, when the pain is on me or on my bairns I call you. It's not to pass the bloody time of day. Whether it's yourself that comes out, or any of your pals from the practice I don't give two tuppenny damns.

'Yes, he says, but it was a question of how busy he was. We had to be careful, he says, but something in his tone of voice got to me. It's been happening rather often lately, he says.

'Well, at that I couldn't help myself. I threw all the blankets off. It was ten stone I'd gone down to, from fifteen, so I was weak but I got the strength back to me. Then, right or wrong, and God forgive me if I did wrong, he was only young after all, but I got up and chased him. He got out of that room fast and me nearly as fast after. He went flying out the door without stopping for his bits and pieces.'

Dan, coughing, brought out the laugh that neither of us could deny.

'And that's not the end of it,' he went on. 'The wife didn't know what was happening with everyone tearing through her kitchen, but she told me off hard for it anyway and was just about kicking me to get back into bed. It wasn't till the next day she told me that the young doctor had come back into the house on tip-toe to pick up his bag. After that it was always someone else who came out from the surgery. I don't think I'd have harmed him very much though.'

As Dan said it, a small bit of movement was coming to that ward. The food-trolley was coming along.

'I suppose I'd better go and take a seat anyway and keep them happy,' Dan said.

'Yes,' I replied and stood up along with him and then said it quickly, something about grapes and stuff, if it was any good to him.

'Thanks boy,' he said, 'And see and get yourself toughened up before I've got another load of scrap ready for shifting.'

That was the sore bit. I suppose it was the dread of how to answer that which had me uselessly fussing over the choice of fruit. Delaying tactics.

'Make it soon.' My own voice said it. That was the nearest I could get to realism.

THE FUNCTIONAL BICYCLE

As a porter in a small-town hospital you tackle a few jobs you would never find in any book of duties. The first time I fiddled with the valve of an oxygen cylinder was like that. You can hardly say it should go to the engineering department when they are all off-shift, so at least ten minutes by car away and the patient is coming back from theatre any time and yes they should have checked for a leak before and should anyway have said their stock in the store cupboard was getting low but... So you forget you know nothing about screws and guages and you shake a few dials and apply the hands, together with the old common sense and then you stand up with your thumbs in the braces of your dungarees and say it's going fine. That should be ten notes, at least, for the trouble: your consultant's fee.

You might also take a look at a blocked sink but you draw the line at drains or toilets.

It is even possible to be requested out away from your seat by the radiator at 3 am and report to the night-sister to be armed with a blood-line and bottle and an elephant-sized syringe and asked if you would do someone the favour of siphoning petrol. Because those people had not planned on making any night-dashes but the coming baby dictated otherwise and it was fifteen miles back and the sister's Mini had a full tank. So you have a moan then a laugh then a mouthful of petrol and spend the rest of the night eating digestive biscuits to try and get rid of the taste.

However, the day the bicycle came in I refused to tackle any repair jobs. That machine looked like it was a stout bit of work but it would need a new back wheel for a start and all right, racing-type bikes were supposed to have drooping handlebars but these were in a sad state. How was the owner?

The nurse explained that the rider was sixty and had come over the handlebars on the only steep hill in the whole area, but his fractured leg would heal all right.

I said I wasn't so sure about an optimistic diagnosis of the bike. So she said thanks anyway and the old soul would be happy if I put a ticket on it and had it stored safely.

For a racing-bike, it was astonishingly heavy. It must have been one of the original models. The fellow must have had a well-put-together frame himself to get away with only a fracture. So I thought as I found an almost vacant corner in the very miscellaneous store.

'Remember that bike?' was the sister's phrase. So that set me up to ask how it was possible to forget it. Then she broke in again:

'You couldn't take it round to the front door for us?'

'So you've fixed himself together?'

'Now you're answering a question with a question,' she said. 'But yes, though it was an awkward fracture, - that's why we had to hold onto him for so long, but he'll be away on the plane today.'

'You're not going to send off that old wreck on the plane - the bike I mean?' I put in.

'We are indeed,' she said. 'So if you can have it round before you take your dinner break - if you could fit that in your hectic schedule?'

As it so happened I really was busy then but she would never have believed me.

'We might just manage that,' was all I said, and so I would have, if the thing had been left where I had put it. I think I did swear when I went through into the store and failed to see that relic. It must have been the thought of having to turn the store upside down that upset me.

The boxes labelled 'Surgical Supplies' could be shifted first. They were bulky but light and so possible to budge. You had to be careful with them though because the containers were of very 'economical' cardboard and prone to burst and of course one of them did, to spill out cardboard urinal bottles by the dozen. The chaos could be sorted later. I would have to get the store in order before the next man came on shift.

Maybe it was him, the other porter, that put the bike away for safe-keeping. Or sold it for scrap or given it to his kids to take apart. But I was sure I had fixed a label on it. Anyway, by the time my relief was come the plane would be gone. Then my eyes went upward to the loft-area.

Getting up there was a bit of an obstacle course, but this was no time to think of approaching the Administration to push for a new step-ladder. The loft was stacked with green plastic buckets and special matching mops: a new design but they were redundant so far because the cleaners all liked the old type better. That old-type bicycle, however, was certainly not up there.

I reported as much to the sister but the fun was over.

'It's only a laugh to you,' she said 'but that poor old soul says he won't go anywhere without his bicycle. Really, the thing means a lot to him. Now, where did you say you put it?'

She went on to ask if there was not another store and what time the other porter came on duty and then suddenly stopped talking and told me I had ten minutes before the ambulance was due to take him to the airport.

I did find it. Or rather one of the engineering boys did, when I put round a plea for assistance. He remembered seeing it in one of the old sheds when he had been looking for something else.

'Which one?'

I was feeling urgency at last and ran to open that shed-door. There were only two things in the place - the defunct fumigation machine with the copper pipes and brass instruction plates; and the old man's made-to-measure cycle, with its solid steel frame and buckled back wheel.

It was over my shoulder in a second, the cycle, not the fumigator, and I ran with it. I made it to the door before the ambulance had even started its engine so there was more than seconds to spare.

I never did see the sixty-year-old-tourer. He was already inside that Bedford and the ambulance driver took charge of the old bike, saying that his union-book made no objections to transporting personal effects. He said thanks and he would put it in the back along with the fellow himself.

No I did not meet the fellow but I did not have to. You can have an idea of someone like that from their machine. He must have been made of quality stuff. There was no way an adventure over the handlebars was going to make him defunct.

DUNCAN

A season is hardly any time at all and so Duncan, who is an uncle of mine, did well to come to us three times in the space of it. Of course 'us' only means 'me'. It's a habit of speech.

Then again he's not really my uncle. I'd better make that clear from the start though you might read things into it since I'm what they call 'unattached'. That's not a good term. Speaking personally, I've got other kinds of family ties. And I've usually enjoyed the jobs I've done. Then reading is something that means a lot to me. I take care over my own dress and appearance and I usually have some baking in the tins in case of people coming in. I can also be competent at little jobs that need doing about the house - but for all these activities I was glad of his coming round, just the same.

Duncan is certainly some sort of a cousin, maybe on my father's side, but not all that old, though his face is what a photographer would call 'interesting'. It was an embarrassed face too, when he showed up at the door, the first time for ages, and said all in a breath that he'd had a bit of luck with his job on a boat and there was a bit of fish going spare so he'd thought of his cousins and was my brother in?

I told him, hadn't he heard, my brother was deep-sea now, catering officer on a tanker, but to come in anyway.

He wasn't going to and then he did but only took his tea standing but he was soon coming out with his laugh. It was the sort you could trust. So I said he was to be sure and come back anytime, fish or no fish, and he wasn't to mind if there was any company in or not. He left a good feeling behind him.

Well of course I went to see what was in the polythene bag - it was one from the mainland, I remember, with the shop's name on it, a big store. It did not contain white fish but prawns and the quality you only see in the big hotels though of course Duncan's offering would have meant just the same supposing it was only a whiting or two.

It was more difficult with Duncan next time. He sat

for a while though he didn't say much and I don't believe we had a laugh once. That made me feel as if he was taking up more of the house. I didn't really mind for myself, only I was worried for his own sake. You notice more in the quiet and I was seeing the red veins standing out from his face.

He said thanks for the tea though he didn't eat anything with it. The bag he left was cold. It was prawns again, and as big as the last lot, but they had been in the deep freeze. Not that it mattered, they taste just the same and I could still take some next door after they were thawed and boiled. It was afterwards I heard that Duncan had lost the job a week or two before that visit, but he was keeping up appearances. I must admit I was annoyed that he felt he had to put on an act here, where he was welcome anyway.

I asked him straight when he came again and he said, yes it was true, but he wasn't bothered, he was out on his own now and here was the catch in the bag. He didn't need any flashy boats now, with a special grant hanging over them. He could still row out far enough to set a few creels.

It was a lobster this time and still alive. That didn't shock me, I've handled them before, in the hotel kitchens, but the black berries disturbed everything. That's what the lobster's eggs look like and that spawn was on this one. The fishermen are supposed to return one like that to the water but some of them scrape the stuff off the shell and sell the lobster as good. That's a waste of the future stock. It would be better that Duncan was honest at least but he had not even noticed the berries. That seems strange. It was as if everything about him was numb. Of course it was obvious to me then, the drink that was in him. He wasn't excited or staggering or anything but I was left feeling sick when he went. And the waste of the black spawn did not help. I couldn't boil the lobster or scrape it but did a worse thing by taking it out the door and opening the dustbin. It fell to the bottom and you could hear it scratching, even with the lid on.

I found out afterwards that this was all on the very day that Duncan went - no that's the wrong word - it sounds as if he died and he did not. Though some said 'disappeared' as if they were making the most of it. Even next door they made a meal of saying how they were dragging the harbour, as if drowning was a judgement from above. I lost patience at that and told them of when I was working at the hospital and once seen a man who'd been taken up from the harbour. I had to help wheel the breathing equipment to be ready at the door. Yes and since I was on duty all night I had to talk to the poor soul that had dived in for him. From Hull he was and the drowned man too. Yes it went that way, though we all tried everything and willed for more.

But what I'm saying is this. What annoyed me was how quickly everyone assumed that our Duncan had gone the same way and it was inevitable since he was an alcoholic who was so often near the sea. The people who make assumptions like that - they would try an oxygen pump all right but they wouldn't have the spirit behind it, not like that crewman from Hull and the doctors themselves. Of course the trawlerman was dead that night but that spirit swung the balance the other way on other nights.

Anyway it turned out that Duncan hadn't ended up in the harbour. He turned up a week after. He'd been going through the horrors away on his own in a hut out on the moor. Not that I'm saying he's cured now. He isn't - but he would have a better chance if people hadn't wanted to say so quickly that he'd fallen in the harbour.

JUBILEE

Yiou could have had the Jubilee for a song. The rot must have been near, though she still looked stately, propped up as she was, in the garden of a bungalow. And that silly structure of hardboard and window-panes as a cabin, but her true line hinting through, for all that. Macleod the Neisach's hand made her hull. No-one else's.

A width to her for two abreast on three beams. Six oars she'd carried, though the bungalow man had installed a violent little engine that thrust an un-natural strain on her timbers. She was built for both the Minch and Atlantic and the meeting of two currents at the Butt of Lewis; but not for engine power.

Ling, codfish and even the halibut were plentiful then, on the great-line. Winter fishing and a big salting afterwards, along the rocks and piers, making the place a little Newfoundland, or Labrador coast. Rich food and high risks. You had to be neat at coming about, dipping the lugsail. Faster yet at tying the reefs, giving the gale less canvas to catch. You had a rough scone, your own barley in it, strengthening the wheat, it all buttered there in your pocket. You gutted whatever had given first blood to the boat and shared out the white livers. Opened your scone. Put in the liver, closed it and sat on the thing till your own heat went through the meal and melted the salt butter into the liver.

I say 'you' and 'your' but I was too young to be risked at that game. I was one of the gatherers of mussels and also took a place in the chain that passed flat boulders out to the launching Jubilee. She was always straining for out but they wouldn't let her go a fathom till the ballast was balanced.

I had my day at the summer-fishing. There were herrings in the sea-lochs, oily in the tide, but all the crews were away again, fighting a war. It was the old men who left their walking sticks behind, fixed up the driftnets and said they'd caught herring before and would do it again. They were one short though it was a smaller craft than the Jubilee. She was already redundant then, needing pitch, shackles and work to do.

So I was to take my place and I wasn't to go asking

my mother. I didn't so out we went. They were all greatly elder than me but made me take a go at a pipe, not long enough to make me sick, but enough to contribute to the clouds that went up into the calm air. They rowed till enough wind came to carry out the sail. The boat listed over a healthy way.

That sail came down when the man who had the best eye or ear or sense of smell or whatever it was discovered the shoals, said they were under the hull. I helped pay out nets. We had not the last one out before the first was near sinking, the buoys weighted down. There was far more herring then the village could eat. There'd be a big price in the town, what with the depleted crews and catches of late.

We landed them and they sold themselves, with their bloody gills and their pearly scales.

I had to take my dram, only one, slowly, but holding it down. They took more but still had great wads of money for home. It was the long way round.

The wind had to hit us and it did. So even the smallest sail we could show was antagonistic to the elements. There was four men to hold her with the oars. It was the tiller for me and I'd to mind and listen and watch for the slightest instruction. I held, listened and watched. I did what I was told and got the feel of it steering, how it worked with or against both waves and oars. There was no time in

our boat or in the sea, that day or night or whenever.

We came in to our own sea-loch and a few things
were still dry in a small kist. The sail took us in and
the oldest man wrote something on a dry bit of
paper and the other three signed it. It was my ticket
of seamanship, they said and I could show it
anywhere.

I showed it later and got out Canada way. Had to
go, because if you're fond of a place you've to get
out and far enough away to see how it fits in the
world. A map's not good enough.

Out north of Vancouver Island, around Prince
Rupbert, the seas were alive., We used half-
salmon as bait to catch halibut. I never thought of
trying to set a halibut to take a whale.

A woman from out own village passed through. Her
man had left our island after two drunken nights.
Some weeks after, we heard she was home-bound,
from the Yukon, with her man on her arm.

And how did I get started on all this? Yes, it was
the Jubilee. I could have bought her myself but I'm
finished now with the seas. No resurgence after
summer herring for me nor for my fellow village
elders. Lesser shoals now, whether it's time for
peace or for war.

But the Neisach Macleod took her back home. He
was a son of the original builder. The cabin took a
deserved toppling and her line was restored. Oiled

shackles and true rope made her fittings and pitch went to her keel. You can see her now at the Port of Ness. Whether you have to drive or walk, sail or swim, she's worth going to see.

IN THE WAKE

You'll find him anywhere, Isle of Lewis to Afghanistan, the man at the edge of the village or town. While he's alive he thrives on friction but people are usually glad to remember him, after he's passed away. Dhol was such a one and he had a verbal hallmark. Before he said anything of significance he came out with a phrase that was his signature. It had no meaning to anyone, except maybe himself. It was probably a corruption of some Gaelic saying but it sounded like, 'In the wake'.

In a temporary spell of peace, Dhol worked with my father on a drifter. He was the cook, but when the nets were not being shot or hauled, the two would be on the deck or in the fo'c'sle, exchanging philosophies. This day, when the wind failed to get near the gale-force, they were on deck, Dhol with the bucket of washing-up. As they debated, he threw the water overboard, and the tin mugs, the forks and spoons, over with it.

My father said he'd seen Dhol talk his way out of a few but this would be one to hear. 'Follow me,' was all the cook said. He went boldly through the wheel-house door and tapped the skipper on the shoulder. Now there was a man who knew Dhol well enough to look for a catch. But this time he couldn't see it when Dhol said, 'In the wake, is a thing lost if you know where it is?'

The only answer he got was an impatient negative, that if you knew the place a thing was in then it couldn't be lost.

'In the wake, there's nothing to worry about, all your cutlery is over the side.'

When the first big war came, Dhol couldn't get as involved in it as most. He jumped from army to navy and back again, often enough, without any permission, official or otherwise, simply to keep an interest. Only once did the Military Police get him face to face.

It was in a Glasgow house, well known as a refuge to Gaelic-speaking people. When the M.P.s approached it a faint line of smoke was coming from one of the cluster of chimneys. The last of a uniform of the Seaforth Highlanders was burning in the grate as Dhol took the staircase down to the street.

They met on the stairs. The two M.P.s had nothing to go on but the name and the birthplace.

'Was there a certain...' and they gave his full, official name, 'up there?'

'In the wake, there was before I left.'

He had told them no lie but it didn't dawn on the M.P.s till they reached the top of the stairs. One was about to give chase but the other held him by the shoulder. He said that a man who came out with a line like that at a time like that, deserved half an hour at least. They never did catch up with him again.

It wasn't only Dhol who had it hard, even after the guns stopped firing for a while. But he decided that his dignity would be helped a good deal by a good suit of clothes. He went in to the tailor on the corner, had the measurements taken and told him not to scrimp with the material. He soon had his suit and was very happy with it.

Some months later, the tailor stopped him in the street, admired the cut of his apparel and said it was good to see that the worry of the debt wasn't lying too heavy on him.

'In the wake,' said Dhol, 'I thought it was quite enough for one of us to be losing sleep over that.'

As with many outcasts and extroverts, Dhol

changed his tack to a religious bearing. He would walk the whole rounds of the Communions, village to village, in a coat that went to his ankles. When seme observant person noticed the same coat in one of the town pubs, the word 'hypocrite' was in his mouth.

Dhol couldn't see it quite like that, it was all fellowship of a kind. But when he met one of the elders of the church, passing outside the door, while Dhol swayed out of the hostelry he seized the chance to speak first. 'In the wake, isn't it a terrible thing that a man in this modern town, has to visit a place like this, to pass his water.'

But eventually it was the poor-house. Under a more updated name of course, but the building was the same. It's easier to accept the outsider after he's dead. Dhol hadn't lost all his spirit.

'Would you happen to have brought a box of Swan Vestas?'

I nodded and passed them to him.

'In the wake, now you'd better give me the Woodbines to go with them.'

I put it to him then, a small plan of writing down some aspects of his life and times, so the stories wouldn't be lost.

'After the wake,' he said. 'Maybe you'd make your fortune but I'd be spending the few days left me in the jail. Time enough to write them down, after the wake.'

3. SMALL TOWN
Cul-de-Sac
A Small Town Man
Aunty Joany
Anna and Mary

CUL-DE-SAC

It was the place I grew up in. I had to remember that when I last revisited the cul-de-sac. This was during my driving test and I was asked to drive past it and reverse back into it. There was no football going on, in the street, at the time but the turn was shakey.

Yet, with the seat-belt off and my body twisted round to facilitate vigilance out the rear window, I caught myself noticing that the fences here were still their same rickety selves. They were composed of thin slats linked only by twists of wire and they tried to separate gardens from pavements. It had been possible to bend them apart the way a gorilla might contemptuously treat the bars of his cage.

The street games had revolved around what

seemed the most northerly lampost, at the far end where the road ended in a wide T. Back at the entrance into the cul-de-sac there was no warning sign of a stubby red road on a longer blue one, all encased within a red triangle, to indicate a dead-end. The two lines of houses met at the outside centre of the bar across the T. It was easy to get in and getting out presented no problems. The examiner did not ask me to reverse all the way back.

Many, including my own family, had got out. Some, like us, had eventually returned to the vicinity, if not to the street.

Others stayed away. Our resident visionary vanished without trace. Her energy of good intentions had attracted me into calling for her daughter. We would go together to school but first I was always offered a bowl of mutton broth and a sermon. Perhaps that mother was a great speaker but she did not have to be, with the elequent head of very red hair. Evening gatherings of like-spirited friends shook the tail of the cul-de-sac with the volume of unaccompanied psalms. She could not last in our street. Her mother and her husband brought up the daughters.

Some never moved away. One of my near-contemporaries now delivers the meat and another the mail. Both can be called upon to cover streets and schemes within a certain radius of their home ground. The fisherman, whose father had tied peacock-herl and grouse hackles into lures, now works with seine-nets. The father's trout had gone next door or across the road but the son's catches reach further. They are iced and sent away in far-outgoing haulage trucks.

Our cul-de-sac produced one television star, but only for a one-off appearance. She was a natural. She had always been a safe neighbour but with a faraway memory of an exile from an even shorter street that had been the only one on her native island. She returned to St.Kilda with other exiles for a commemorative service which was televised. These people had various traces of accents. Most remembered which end of their ruin had held the fire and which the bed. Most thanked the Lord they had been removed from that place. Our neighbour was spontanious, not practical, but Im glad she said that if someone would repair the roof on number three, she'd return tomorrow.

Back in our cul-de-sac, a very thin boy who had not been expected to survive a fall from a roof became a cross-country champion, in the army.

The most promising footballer we produced eventually stopped running from kitchen-job to kitchen, fleeing from city to city. He stayed put in a village fifteen miles from the town and makes solid leather goods with gold-leaf burnished in. This is done with the aid of brass tools, given him by a city book-binder.

We had an artist. He won his regular way through

the age-group sections of national competitions. In early days the results appeared in newspapers. We saw them in print during meal-times. This was after being shouted in and away from the number and arrow and question games that commenced from that same habitual spot on the T. When the television came we did not need so much per-suasion to enter our houses. Then we saw the artist's name, under his work, still winning compe-titions. One of our immediate neighbours had one of the canvases in his living room. He was a joiner and had bought it or else traded it for work or wood. The artist went on through college and then had exhibitions in various art-centres. I never saw any of them. My family had moved away by then and so were naturally a bit out of touch. There is no new work to view, now. He never looked in the least anaemic, having a wrestler's beard rather than a wispy one. He died very young.

Our scientist doubtless had to work for his eminent position but it was generally known from the start that he would achieve his research fellowship at Oxford. He is robust and returns only in the winter, bringing an ice-axe and crampons home with him. He made the mistake of letting it slip to his parents that people working with radiation could not realis-tically expect to survive sixty. He would do fine if he got well into his fifties.

We had two businessmen, living at the extremities of one side of the central street that went up towards the bar of the T. They rose in disconnected ventures and both crashed most completely when they seemed on their most winning line. One got half a hold on a city pub for island exiles. The other kept local with a lemonade factory to fill bottles and send out to children and to old ladies to give to children along with buttered cream-crackers. And to alcoholics who had managed to beat the more misty bottle. Both businessmen are survivors. They may not rise so high again but they will not go jumping out of any windows

More recently, two daughters from the same house both survived in an area of Italy that was desecrated by an earthquake.

It may seem that this spectrum is a fake light; too broad for the perimeters of the T. shape. Or that I am seeing the street in an imaginary and over-rich light, despite failing my driving-test in it. The place is real. Some of these people lived under the same roof. I have not classified them, door to door, in family groupings. So the artist and the scientist were brothers and the woman from St. Kilda and the cross-country runner are mother and son.

These are the certainties but the cul-de-sac has also produced possibilities. It may have reared two writers. If anyone reads this they may see the results of my own pencil-marks, after the red pen and the typewriter have taken their turn.

The other potential writer came out into the open at the Bridge-Club dinner. I sat opposite her and was forced into honesty when she asked what I was doing, if anything, these days. It was difficult, seated there in the torquoise shadow of the hotel's new curtains, to admit that my only aspiration was to write well. I must have looked far from Bohemian in a suit and tie.

A silence after my statement was very short and concerned only us. The rest of the table was involved in other sections of conversations. She talked first of what her surviving son was doing and then cut across her own tack to tell me she had filled several exercise books with some memories and thought of going back sometime, to see if they made any sense. It was a question of finding enough space around you, wasn't it?

Yes and getting a workmanlike attitude to meet with the sheer need.

Maybe her office took up more time than she could afford but she needed the outlet more than the money.

Yes, sometimes the space between the walls of your room seemed to shrink. You put shelves up, trying to imply more height as a compensatory factor. You reared a large dog which needed walking and reminded you to get out of the house. There had been several changes of address since leaving the cul-de-sac but it didn't seem possible to attain such balanced proximity with your neighbours.

The waitresses were coming round again to take

our main-course plates away. Mine was empty, so I must have been eating as I was talking. Hers was not. We talked on. When it came to the sweet-course, which was the clinching one, she passed her unfinished pudding across the table to me. I was able to get to the bottom of that bowl.

A SMALL TOWN MAN

He said he was not willing to generalise and say that characteristics belonged to groups, whether the Arabic nation or the travelling gypsies but he remembered a few individuals all right. Some things you had no choice about coming to mind. Wanting to recall or forget did not come into it.

In Egypt, war time of course, - he could not say exactly how it came about, but he found himself being welcomed at some home-fire out there. The stew-pot was on the boil and so was his own anxiety. He had never been able to fight his own stomach. He knew it was sinful to refuse an offering but he thought he would have to disgrace himself. He always recoiled against unfamiliar food though he could say that another man's colour or costume had never bothered him.

Then he sneaked a glance at the stew and the sheep's eyes stared back. A comic set-piece - but that was all right. He was re-assured and could happily eat this stuff. The half carcass was in there: food for a few families and this was not so strange. If he had not quite been reared solely on sheep's head broth it was nothing new to him. So when they had heaped a bowl with some of the shoulder he did not have to act out his gusto. The spices and so on were maybe foreign but the Arab's sheep had the same anatomy as their own and the shoulder, well-stewed, was as good a bit of it as any. Mind though, any ricey-stuff would have thrown him. He would have had to refuse the meal and the culture that was being held out to him.

And he could never accept their syrupy coffee but when they spoke in English he could relish their talk. In fact, if he had been out there a bit longer he might have set about picking up a bit of Arabic. He was placed back nearer home sooner than he would have guessed. The war was going on but the doctor reckoned he would be in as much danger from travelling as from bullets.

So he did not go back overseas to the war but it came to him - in bomber planes. He was put on watch with a strong-featured man. The lads all called him Red Tinker but the man was simply 'Angus' to him. They would talk the night away when they had the chance. Angus had always been an outdoor man. This dark-watching shift was nothing to him.

One night Angus had laid a heavy hold on his arm and said he had seen a shadow, way-up. You would have sworn that nobody could have seen anything but the stars. Crisp night it was - the sort you might almost expect the Aurora.

Angus insisted something was up there so they got on the blower and sure enough the fighters went up.

The commendation came, soon after. Great feat it was, they said, to spot the bomber at that height. Almost unbelievable, they said, without equipment. The story was out, how Angus had the eyes for it. Outdoor narrow ones. He'd seen the shadow, as he said, blocking a star.

Angus was shifted then. He was posted down where they could best use his vision - down to where the bombers hoarded over. Angus could spot them all right - a good man to have around - but how long would he have lasted down there?

There had never been any news. Angus was not a man for writing letters. So there was no way of knowing. Maybe that was why he came back so strong now. The praising of Angus had maybe cost Angus dear.

You could talk to him about culture all right as long as you let him remind you it was only one side of things. He went for a bit of it still, he said, through to the city, though he would always be essentially a small-town man. Yes he would have himself a scrub and a quick tea when he finished work and then he'd be away in the Volvo. Not often mind - but if there was a half-decent play he might fancy. Not the very modern stuff though, and Shakespeare he reckoned, was still as good as any of them.

As for the rest of it, art-galleries and all, he didn't bother much with them now. He said he'd long since seen his share of paintings. In the war. Florence. It was an Army course: recreation for the boys. Yes he signed on for an Art-tour. There was no football that day, so why not? He remembered a few of the works still. The brightness surprised him, he remembered. You'd have thought the Old Masters would be all dull and reverend-like. No fear.

It was back to Blighty as they'd put it though it sounded pretty dated now. The same small-town for him, then. Everyone had known him as a footballer and a layer of paths and a maker of sheds or gates or whatevers - and willing to shove a pen or push a shovel or do whatever was on the go. Only nothing was going. All his contacts said that things were very quiet just then, pal, but that's how things go - and we're all still mates of course.

That was when he started up on his own. Desperation, you could call it. Selling Insurance. But you were sleeping with other people's money under your pillow. Or trying to. He couldn't. It was either a breakdown or getting clear of that.

The job on the mechanical side came up then: he could thank the skies for that. All right, it might sound even greasier than handling pound notes. Bits of engines, sure but you see where the pieces have to fit, even if you're only cleaning them. You pick up the parts and you pick up the knacks.

Yes that line was doing him all right, even now. Lads weren't bad to work with. Only thing that bothered him was the attitude to the Union. Not that he minded knocking his pan in on his own, seeing to correspondence, conducting two-man meetings with the treasurer. But what the union meant to most of the boys was the few bob deduction. They gave their dues all right but you never saw their faces - only looked up the union-man if they cut their hand and had a claim to make.

Like he said, he didn't get them down for that but - you know - after all the years it took, and all the muck they'd had to shift to get the channels open. Labour and management. So a fair deal could work both ways. Had to. So you took your pride into the job and into picking up the brown envelope at the end of the week. Yes and so it was worth collecting.

It had to work both ways. You could call that keeping the human touch or the channels open. And wasn't that what he started on saying. Your plays and paintings were trying after the same thing weren't they? The old human contact.

Anyway, even admitting all the things that could sicken you about the old town, he reckoned you probably had more chance of keeping a human face there. Cities for him were things to visit and then come back from.

AUNTY JOANY

Don't you be so condescending about my aunties,' Mary-Jane said. 'I'm very fond of them, I'll have you know. But one especially. The other two are sweet enough, but this one, Aunty Joany, she's got something...'

So Mary-Jane, though she had her coat on now, sat on her desk and delayed her get-away. She had quite a lot to say about the house she was bound for.

The place was saturated with gentile sweetness. The main room had a bit of a bathroom about it with its pot-pouri potions. This was too tasteful a house for any flying ducks, but the walls were heavy with china, as plaques and in cabinets and mostly as rosy as the teacups.

Tea was a ritual. Cloths and napkins came from a drawer to their places. Patterns to all; for all...

Not quite. Two aunts fitted into everything and everything was fitted to them. It was all revealed on a two-tiered tea-plate. One aunt could coax up a sponge-cake with delicacy; another showed her savoury touch. The third aunt sat aside a bit. She was the only one of the three that Mary-Jane gave a name to: Joany.

She was not so out of things, claiming a share of the cake though she hardly had need of the conversation. She had plenty of her own and not exactly one-sided. She had Moppa and Robina. Joany and that pair had an unabashed plenty to say for themselves. The other two aunts would have been openly scandalized if they had not been so polite.

'Childish' they thought of their older sister, as if it were an insult. But they were practised at containing, despite the mumblings of the eccentric Joany. Her and her imaginery 'Moppa' and 'Robina'! She was not quite capable. Of course it was a shame in a way, her being out of touch.

She was not. Moppa and Robina could not be seen but they spoke of real things. Joany knew what was what in the world. She must have done. She went to the Americas.

There was no holding her back and not for the want of trying. Joany had always wanted to cross an ocean, so she flew to Honolulu. By Jumbo-jet.

Safely. And back again, but breaking the journey in New York, stopping off to do some shopping.

A big city that, as she afterwards said to her imaginary friends. But there was good and bad wherever you went. And the same with Honolulu, for all its palm trees. And Moppa and Robina thought so too.

The real-life aunts of Mary-Jane shook their heads as sister Joan. How she had managed... on her own... they could not imagine... all that distance.

They could not imagine, as Mary-Jane said, buttoning her coat.

ANNA AND MARY

The only surviving Volkswagon Beetle in this Hebridean town gave a hiss of breath and stopped dead, three metres from the gangway. A girl toppled out first and stood up tall in a short yet snug jacket. She had a brown roll clinched between her teeth. It might have been the start or finish of her breakfast.

The male driver found his way out next and pulled a second passenger by the arm till she came out the door with a flourish and then a paler gesture of exhaustion. Doors were left wide open. Both girls carried their own neat back-packs while the man smothered his physique under a clutch of carrier bags that had to be held at the bottom. The firmly positioned gangway had safety rails on either side.

There would be few other travellers this morning. It was a strange time of year to go gallivanting to or from the Island. So there were seats to choose from and vacant space in the luggage compartment, outside the lounge. Anna and Mary stowed their own packs and their companion deposited all their miscellaneous extras. Leaning back against the nearest bulwark, Anna, the taller of the two girls, spoke first.

She did not go on to any conclusion after her 'but'. This Island was different, you had to say, from your expectations and from any other place you'd ever been but...

And David, the man with the thick hair not quite under control and the unshaven produce of several days, had to try to remember where Anna had said she'd been. Africa. No, that was Mary. Anna had once spent some time on a Navaho Indian reservation.

Neither of them, he thought, were of the merely curious kind: those travellers who look at artefacts of the area as if there is a semi-visible glass partition somewhere or other between the eye and the object.

Anna was confident, but a listener as well as a talker. Neat with it. This was her usual long-legged stance, in relaxed cord jeans. Her moderate weight went evenly to the flat, wide shoes with bright red uppers. Mary seemed a girl of fresh-printed dresses. The one she was wearing at that moment trailed boldly, in quiet flair, down from the woolen hem of her classic coat. She did not often look quite as relaxed as Anna but could surprise you. Her hand would come down with a thump on your forearm and then keep lightly there with a downward weight as she put firm but very quiet emphasis on whatever point she was making at the time.

Their last spell of travelling had been in very different locations, far from home, at the same time. They had both independently worked-out the letters to parents, extending the month into three. Then Mary had written a more difficult explanation of why her journey had to last nearer the year's length. Anna had been horrified, confronted with New York as a stopover on the way back. Mary had been more gradually prepared for the return. She had described how villages in the more prosperous parts of Nigeria had tin roofs as a flourish of wealth. These were impractical, teasing an already provoked sun. She preferred to look back to the earlier villages that could teach urban planners worldwide a thing or two. Red clay huts were roofed in the stuff that grew in the area and the overall designs held a fine tension between family privacy and social channels.

Both girls had known well that an extension of stay was impossible this time. That old man they were working for, back in Dublin, was very far from being an ogre but he would be already fidgeting in in his seat. Amongst other secretarial stuff, they typed out the stories he had written out in long-hand. He too had travelled in his day - but no, that wasn't fair. This day was as much his as anyone else's. He didn't retreat or depend too much on inspiration but worked steady hours and apologised for asking them to retype something he'd re-hashed. He would first look up at them and then, more slowly, put his hand to the classy tin caddy of large-leafed tea, when he'd thought they'd had enough, or too much, deciphering for the moment. Then he'd let loose a few opening lines, calculated to set his two secretaries talking. A man of charm.

David now made a show of aiming his head at his feet and saying he was jealous.

He was born in the wrong environment surely. Did he just want people all around, anticipating his wishes? That was Mary's pretended response.

No, no, they had him all wrong.

It was Anna who first relented, remembering how they had just been treated to baker's brown rolls. Gleaned from the Lord knows where at five o'clock of an unearthly morning. And here was themselves fed and delivered in good time for this vessel. There was no holding the sentences together at this time of day, but for all his macho fungus the man was something nearly... Was gentle the word? Comparatively speaking.

He was full of surprises though. It was Mary's turn. Revealing how organised he was in his unlikely environment of harmony and taste, set somewhere in the middle of this living Hebridean town which was a planner's nightmare. There was very good contrast in his room with the bamboo slats diagonally across the glass, trailing plants suspended from it. That was original, but as good a way as any of making use of an old fishing rod.

And he'd never told them where exactly the hand-woven hangings were made, far less taken them to meet the maker.

In fairness he'd taken them instead to where the road ends and the rhythmic seams in the cliffs have the same energy in them as the sea. They'd arrived to glimpse that coast in the dusk, too late in the day to risk a venture across the wind-beaten shore. But they must have walked in an Atlantic storm before this visit. And Anna had gone soaring in his estimation since she'd stolen the V.W. She'd gone speeding off for a lot more than the hundred yard token effort. So he and Mary had first tried to sprint then slowed, being careful of their step across the machair grasses in what was left of the light.

It was what you might call a bit of a change from Dublin.

They didn't spend all of their days in the city? He'd a friend once who'd done the lot, P.H.D. and all, in Aberdeen. They kept offering him more research to do but he eventually found out how to say no. He only wanted to work on an oilrig long enough to get some money, then he'd be off to set up a second-hand bookshop in Dublin.

There were dozens of the like there, people who'd escaped. And what about himself? Was he sailing with them now or what? The V.W. would be handy on the other side. Could he not take a wrong turning and drive it down the ramp? They'd need the transport to take all the bundles of wool they were carrying.

That lot had come from their own hard bargaining. Anna proof-reading and Mary typing his special report that was overdue, while he cooked dinner for them and it had to be fish. He'd taken care to prepare it in a blend of tradition and cross-cultural influence: oven baked with leeks and dill. And him running to and fro sorting out the oddments of wool but keeping a part of his attention on the oven. He had gained that wool when a broke client had paid him in goods for a special job.

That particular bargain didn't seem too different from the Irish way of doing things. Mary said that. But barter and banter aside for a second, it had been a great trip.

David rubbed the growth on his chin and said, joking aside, if the bosses would swallow the story, he'd still have his weight on the boat when the gangplank did not have its own. When the ropes were loosed from the pier.

Would there be a stink?

There would. His reputation might survive intact for an hour while they thought he was behind his door after an early start. But the first client or even the prolonged silence would give the show away. One of the senior partners would be delegated to negotiate the spiral stair to the top floor, knock and enter. The grey filing cabinet would be as dead as a drawer in a morgue. The rather good, leather inlayed desk would be spread with emptiness before the window that surveyed the jumble of rooftops. No, there might be a three-quarters empty carton of milk gone sour and Hell, his books might be visible. Only two paperbacks. 'Dubliners' and the selected poems of one Seamus Heaney, but enough to damn him by their presence in office hours. It would look as if he never did any work between brief interviews with the few clients assigned to him. A sudden thought. Did the Irish do nothing but write and talk?

It might be better if that were true.

However.

David cast a furtive glance back to the pier. The gangway was still in position. He knew there had never been any doubt of that. But maybe they'd be back over. He said that, even as he dared to consider the possibility that only one of the girls would feel the most pressing need to return. Maybe that would happen even before he could visit Dublin as promised.

There could be minutes or even half an hour before

the ferry left. It was still called 'sailing' even now that the days of steam had given way to diesel engines. It was pointless to delay. He did not try to embrace either Anna or Mary but made a mime of panicking at the prospect of that gangway going. He took the safe way down it.

The doors of the Beetle were still open. Frost was efficient in keeping you alert. A flamboyant but much needed scarf was wrapped once around the neck area of a quiet shirt and equally conservative V-neck sweater. He was glad he'd left his suit jacket at home, even though he now shivered. It would all too soon be necessary to collect it along with his tie, and also have a shave before work. There was not much point in trying to sleep for an hour or two, in car, couch or in bed. He'd drive a mile from town, walk around a bit, then return to do those necessaries.

Then it would have to be up the stairs. He would wedge a window open, perhaps using the paperbacks. Better let a breeze go through the room. It would not be so easy to keep on the ball now that the stimulation of the last few days was ebbing. Restoration to routine.

Keys dangled from the ignition switch. He had confidence in his battery and he'd seen to his plugs and points. The engine started first time. No matter which route the vehicle would try to take, its eventual stopping place was inevitable. Meanwhile its driver could play with the idea of Mary's return from off the same gangplank. This action would be performed quite slowly because of these floating dresses she wore.

But this morning the wheels would have to sound on the mundane gravel of the office car-park. Its driver would climb the spiral to confront the smell of sour milk. In over-quiet or harassed moments he could consider Dublin as a city to work in. There were booksellers in plenty but maybe he could continue his own line in a different office. Or maybe he had to think of crossing oceans. Mary still had a faraway gaze.

Anyway, what was all the urgency about and where was it coming from? The house was at last very nearly as he wanted it and the car was running well. Yet the links were there for the using. Telephone wires had long since crossed both the Minch and the Irish Sea.

Then again, nothing was certain. There had been no explicit statements. If he was the master of his own fate, she was the mistress of hers. And didn't she know it, the same girl who had gone to Africa.

The wheels were turning out of town at a pace which took account of the possibility of ice. Its driver had to make sure of an eventual return. There were several messes to sort out. Stale milk was the least of them. What you really had to worry about was the sort of problem that festered in businesslike folders.

So he would work late tonight and all this week, catching up, but within easy reach of the telephone. The wires might well connect with Dublin if he sommoned enough commitment to dial the numbers.

4. LETTERS
Letter
Air-Mail
Surface Mail and Above

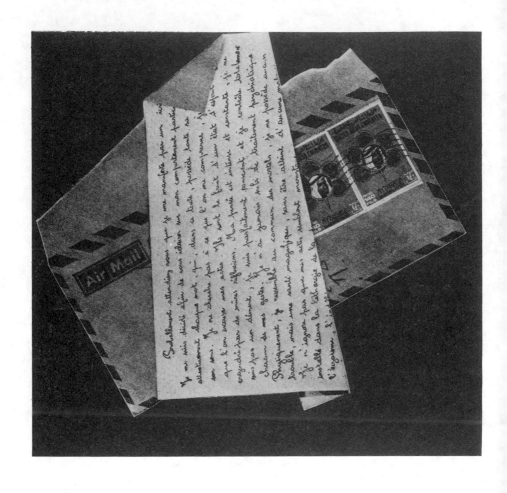

LETTER

I will trust you, dear one, not to mind any nostalgia or sentiment in what I'm remembering about when you came over to us. You slept a whole day and woke to inform me you'd had enough of sitting and **being travelled** by ships and wheels. Now you wanted to walk on strong. Then you were a bit bashful and added 'only if it would be alright with you.' I said it would be much better than alright. You smiled with a question-mark on top of your head. You were not so sure of the language then.

So we took the walk out, the shore way and went by a man who would not pass us without a word. You were not sure how to take his admiration of your tassled hat. You wanted to give it away to him. The poor man would have been embarrassed.

It was already sandy before the path faded out. You could hardly believe in what you saw. 'But you called it a shore. This is a good beach,' you said and I said maybe. You asked if people swam here. Yes, I used to - Yes it was cold. Always. No thank you, I did not want to swim today.

We did not swim. We did not hold hands. We were close, though, in looking out over the coily patterned sands, across the cold shallows to Broad Bay. 'The best haddock-fish came from there,' I said. You asked why it was 'came' in the past tense and not 'come'. 'Bigger boats with bigger nets or just the times, changes,' was all I could offer. 'But surely there must be some of those fish left,' you said. I said 'the stragglers' and did not try to explain.

We walked on but not far, only to the solid ribs left from a wide, buxom boat. Our Island designs had little of the Viking in them: no long, tough narrow lines to our small boats. And no sign of the brown, dipping-lug sail that would have once hung over her. But we could still shelter in her body and we did touch then, both putting a hand out to the transom of the stern which was still holding the timbers, joining them. We trusted each other to notice how the rudder was askance, redundant and unsteering, nearby in the sand, flaking into it.

Something made me remember then, the living bit of wood I still had round the blade of a fisherman's knife. I only had to fish as deep as my pocket for it and showed it and told you proudly of the bigness of the man who had placed that knife in my palm as a gift.

We were ready for the return. It was the coldest day of summer. It made me hungry and for more than cold food - though, yes, your Switzerland style salads, dressed in cream and mustard, were better than good. You proved that later. Your flavours went well with our island stuff even though you could not get hold of all your herby ingredients.

Hot food did not yet await us. But then when we went into the kitchen there was a bundle of papers on the table. You asked what was in it. We un-wrapped it together and unveiled the grey fish that they say is blessed with the thumb - mark of Peter, a haddock but a beauty of a one. So then I could admit that maybe someone I knew had been out on Broad Bay and taken his basketful, the first for years, the real fish.

I took the knife to it and you shuddered. The head was left on and the white liver was taken, to be mixed with oatmeal and stuffed in the head. You were horrified but the only way to cook it was this way and whole like a salmon, but in the milk with leeks.

You were sad at the head with opaque eyes staring up at you, as you said. Yet you ate. You ate from it all, everything here and not just so you could say you had tasted our traditions.

That is why I think of you now and say how you moved me and move me. You share in the life of the people you meet and mourn the death of more than fish.

Come back with us now. Come home to me.

AIR-MAIL

The second or third opening phrase which occurred, my American Friend, was this one:

'It was a good day for eggs.'

The above attempt may contain an element of surprise but could only work the vein of our relationship which contents itself with banter. Right now I want to recall the day on the cliffs when we got further. But what has all this got to do with eggs? Read on, friend, and as much will be revealed as my honesty will permit.

I cannot deny that our first meeting point was in fast and light talk over coffee. Right from the second week of term. Familiarity in the first week would have been asking too much, bearing in mind our fabled native reserve. Yet we did make it past the shallow, verbal-exchange stage, even before the day of the big, final outing. However, this analysis is becoming unsettling and is affecting more than my letter-writing style. It is sounding too close to sociological jargon, which is worth less than banter, in anyone's language. So friend, I want to stop watching myself writing and get close to you by remembering the meeting that led to our day together.

We both had a share in a sharp burst of open talk, in the cafe at the edge of the cobblestones. You drank tea because all the diatribes about the quality of coffee served up in Britain had so far proven true. Your cup was forcefully drained and returned to the saucer, as you spoke of having to **address** a flag in the mornings of your childhood. That word you used had nothing to do with posting letters. I returned this by stating how our class-room experience necessitated an early-morning chorus of parrots, with eyes down to the book of dogma.

Three or four others, seated at the same table, became involved in what ensued. The two plump women at the counter stopped squeezing out teas and coffees into transparent cups and shook their heads. This level of animation in their morning customers was unusual. Perhaps we all also betrayed an undertone of self-consciousness at continuing discussions outside a seminar: acting as students are reputed to, but rarely do.

Come to think of it, you and I reinforce stereotype images of the fair, American, blue-eyed male and the ginger, Scottish fellow, but we cannot help that. Bringing heads together is important.

It must have been this opening of ourselves in the cafe which made you decide to offer me a share in your last day's gasp of unabashed tourism. And which prompted me to accept. You steered and I navigated our hired-car out of the city and beyond the suburbs. We left it when it had brought us within walking distance of the cliff-area. I had been there once before.

Those coastal houses hardly even comprised a village. They were loosely gathered round the prescribed yet nevertheless valid and calm things: little church, old cemetery, real inn and pier with creels. Until we achieved the harbour breakwater, all the old stone-work remained out of our reach: dykes and gravestones and ale-houses. This had nothing to do with gates or opening times. There were no signposts to bear prohibitions. But we were too busy saying how befitting everything was and worthy of the description: 'neat'. Neither of us could reach a finger out to touch the walls. Not before the pier. I don't know why things went so quiet there. We even noticed the smell from the few threads of fish's remains that were left drying in the nets.

The walk out along the cliffs, up from the harbour, slowed us completely. We talked, but not fast. We discovered that both of us had grandfathers worthy of the name and when one of us suddenly asked without embarassment if the other believed in God, there was no pause before 'Yes' then: 'Me too.'

Sea-birds were as many and strong on the rocks and sea below as up above out heads. I was trying to remember the word for things or people wanting to crowd together. 'Gregarious', you said. That was our teaching for you, was my reply, and surely a cue for a wisecrack. We had drunk-in the serious stuff in one slow, long gulp about faith and families so it was ripe time for lightening the air.

It didn't work out that way. We were remembering the Hitchcock film. You'd been to the place where they'd made it and there still was an unnerving lot of birds there. And here.

I saw the eggs then, as the ducks flew up. There was four in her nest. 'Fat ones,' I put it. You didn't look exactly horrified, but getting that way. Your reaction somehow urged me further into my assumed role of unromantic man of the soil.

'One of these would make an omelette and it's not as if there's any shortage of ducks round here.'

You just quietly replied that you weren't so sure of incubation times but then gave me a hand while I dared out over the edge. Guilt must have touched me even then because I fingered and shook two eggs before taking a decisive grip of one. When we were again a step back from the cliff I proclaimed that there was an element of suffering before any kind of eating. I may even have glanced back towards the three eggs left in the nest. The feel of the shells had told me nothing but there was now one egg as a gleaning and a trophy in my woolen hat. Still warm and held out in my hand.

We moved on. Our boots really did walk by a host of daffodils even though the blooms sprung from a ploughed field. Soon they would be for sale in a city shop. Then the drive back had to come. That car was bright yellow too, come to think of it.

You offered to return it later. You still had to pick up one or two things: preparations for the big departure. We both got out before my door and shook hands there. Of course we played it down and said we'd see us when we saw us. Hardly even waved.

I went up slowly towards my room but stopped at the top of the stairs. The hat was still in my hand but held at my side while I tried to open the door. Wetness came to my skin as the handle turned and I looked first in my hat and saw the cracked mess that had the early signs of a young bird's form in it. Some moments beat past before I lifted the wool of my sweater and had to look at the stain that the broken egg had left on my white shirt. This was more red than yellow.

Blood doesn't bother me all that much, it's not

Living at the Edge

that, but it took me along by the snout back to a loud voice about the elements of suffering which I know very little about.

Look, I realise this is a strange sort of thing to write about but will send you this letter. We cannot have anything less than honesty now: not after the pier and the cliffs where we got further than the banter.

SURFACE MAIL AND ABOVE

K halid, your parcel must have made it intact to my gate. But not as far as my door. I followed the trail of pieces of padded envelope and found my beret clinging to the rosebushes. Thanks for sending it on. I knew I'd left it nowhere else. Your small envelope came next to hand though it was my sister that had retrieved it earlier and set it to wait on the mantelpiece. The letter was intact. I was hungry and smelly in a very unfeminine fashion after the very rural sort of day that is a reaction against a term of study - but I tore into your words before even trying to trace all the strange threads of ripped parcel that were littering our garden.

Your writing is like your talking. The English is of

course excellent but with an unorthodox something or other which the native speaker is incapable of. Your flow is under the spell of a very aware consciousness - most of the time - and I can see you've been reading that book I sent. Its prose gets like poetry does it not? And reveals the feel of rooting and growing, reacting and conflicting and all such things that are big and strong in this small country of ours. Next, the post will bring you the work of one of our more Northern and rural poets, but unsentimentalised of course, because you know how I feel about fairy worlds - airy or otherwise!

In turn, that poem you translated took me along as you knew it would. It is so strong in the simple way that keeps you from wanting to say how it is so deep. 'Wings' is the word for what it does.

Then, yes, you remembered how the Arabic chanting struck me like Gaelic and the mosque-mosaics like the Book of Kells. You had one volume showing blue ceramics and interlocking white letters. I had the other, opened out alongside with illustrations of the illuminated manuscripts in golds and reds, all fair woven in. These calligraphers and monks must all have been patient men.

Your next reference surprised me. You found these little mushrooms you said and remembered seeing a picture somewhere, along with a promise of certain 'properties'. Maybe I would like to try them. No Khalid, you have me wrong there. I may be unorthodox for a student of medicine but I don't go around swallowing everything organic that comes to hand or mouth or through the garden gate. Camomile tea is one thing, lemon balm is fine but these fungus things are not so kind to the mind.

No, I'll stop going on about it or you'll think this is a sermon of a letter. We only know some of what moves each other but we can work on it - what say you? We can write back and fore and clear of the swaying of attitudes and feelings which are even bigger moves than yours of flying to study in Glasgow. Or mine of crossing over from the South and up to the boat at Larne. That is the way you have to come if you are serious and jaunty enough to meet our culture full in the face. You will be welcome at our house, and if your father and brothers would have premature heart-attacks and strokes and all at your palming out chapatis to teach me the knack, my mother is going to faint to see a man trying to mix buttermilk into the dough for the soda-bread.

Yes, Khalid, and though it might take me a while to attain the Hymalayas or even the Kashmir Mountains I was up our own hill an evening, a night and half a day - and all between your package and this reply. Oh, and I wore the beret up. It was an old friend back, torn from travels, but maintaining character and distinction. Even its crowning pip was gone. But more of that later, as they say.

I have been up that way before but the mood is different with the company. We were three and the labrador dog. The calves of our legs were shouting out but the only other stimulation we needed was milk chocolate - it beats your honeyed sweetmeats. The clouds were so fast, over us and the rocks, that we spoke of Tibet but John and Isobel, the Scots settlers - you'll meet them I hope - they were dreaming practically enough to reckon out the air-fare but potently enough to say they would spend all their savings to propel themselves to the Indias.

Yes and we were already in the heights. The summit was rocky and the power was there and the strangest of lichens and mysterious mosses. But no mushrooms, Khalid, none for us. The sky had colour enough for any and all when we rounded the shoulder of the hills. The last light caught lochans of water down below and the first of the moon was crescent as a symbol. This was the place for tea and rest.

The only apparatus we needed was the original brass model of a stove which John produced from its tin box, along with a sacred bottleful of fuel. We performed the operation from our sleeping bags, all nestled on a polythene sheet.

The minature stove was as strong as a steam engine when you pumped air into its heart. It bellowed to boil the water and we all loved its energy. The water hit the leaf of Darjeeling which had come via our village supermarket. The stuff hissed well.

It was easy to imagine the tea growing by the rock

by the stove... Yes I know you could see the mush-rooms growing there too, but plants in nature can be calming or poisonous just as the potions that man manufactures.

So thanks for the thought, really, of sending those things but when we do climb together it will be to the hills of Ireland or Scotland or else to the Kash-miri Mountains by way of a cheap, student flight on a jet-plane. - Oh I nearly forgot to say where your fungi did go.

After devouring your letter I returned to follow the pieces of chewed-up envelope down past the rose-bushes where our labrador-pup must have torn the pip off the beret, but missed the inner envelope of your letter which my sister had recovered. The dog could not have missed your mushrooms though. There was no sign of them along the trail, but only by implication, in the animal's behaviour. These fungus things do not simply evaporate, not even when digested by man or dog.

In this case it was definitely dog. The beast had the disorientated look about him for more than a day.

5. **COLIN**
    Compost
    The Move
    Misfits

COMPOST

olin said he was selling the Austin. This came out when I was sitting up front on one of the seats he had covered in tweed. He noticed me glance to the back seats, which he had brought back to life with leather polish, and he knew that I was also considering the unseen repairs plus the hours he had spent under the chassis of the thing.

'You're thinking she and I have been together for a while and how could we part?' It was not a question. I did manage a sort of laugh. Then he added, 'I suppose it really is a sort of betrayal. She was quality - is quality - after all. Worth putting the work into her. You know the feeling when you're building on something solid.'

Colin turned the corner with finesse and we went up the road to the house he had built. Out front, the bonnet of the Austin gleamed in the first sun after rain. She was almost like the old black sedan: pure style.

The brake was on. We paused before the gate.

'You know of course this was to be the very last move,' Colin said. I nodded, remembering my first meeting with Colin and Sarah. They were then freshly established in the living room of 'Greenhill'. It had a comfortable austerity with a stone fire place and clean-cut lines of furnishings. Colin had chosen the materials used throughout the house. He had supervised all the building but also acted as mason on his own hearth. They had not wanted anything ostentatious. Colin had been proud of the mantelpiece timber; part of a builder's plank which had been rescued from its function of steering wheelbarrows over mud. He had taken the blueprints out from a drawer and I was impressed with how the aesthetic simplicity, sought in the drawings, had been achieved in the building.

'Well we'd better head in,' Colin said. Our pause had allowed him to roll a cigarette. 'I did arrange it with the new owner,' he added. 'It's all right of course.'

So we had permission to enter the garden of the house which Colin had designed for his own retirement. We did so, bringing our tools from the boot. I had the fork, he had the sacks. This was the first time I noticed that Colin's full height was only about equal to my own. Perhaps it was his lean frame and rather gaunt face, or else the sheer neatness of even his working dungarees, and tweed jacket, that normally gave his seventy-year-old figure the impression of strength.

'I'm not denying he is a fine, courteous, sensible and upright man, this one who has bought over Greenhill. But he has no interest in growing things. I can't understand that.'

The lawns were gone. Rustling grasses had taken over. The roses in the front beds looked a bit out of hand to me, but to Colin they were finished. 'Black Spot,' he stated, and I could not avoid the echo from Hardy: 'The rotten rose is ripped from the wall.' This was all a bit much for me. All aspirations to perfection were gone from this garden but there were still signs of thriving life. The fates were not as large as that life to me but what could I say from my stance of twenty-odd years.

We continued along the path to the back garden, prepared to dig out the last of Colin's sacred compost, which would be shifted down to his son's house.

'Even the tits have deserted the place.'

I could hardly deny sympathy to that, even on this fine Saturday of early Autumn sun. I managed to notice that the rough but neat little bird tables and shelters were bare of either food or birds, and already looked very neglected. The vegetable beds, a few paces away, could only just be made out from the overgrowth. Feathery greenery made the carrots recognisable and there were a few green needles nearby which suggested onions underneath.

'Waste,' Colin said. I was nearer the patch so bent over and pulled one carrot. It was firm and good. The words were in my mouth, something about at least taking the remaining vegetables home because that new owner would never use them, but I managed to swallow the suggestion. It would have jarred against something or other.

But since the carrot was in my hand I rubbed the earth off on my shirt and bit into it. Colin in turn managed a smile at that before we set to the digging and bagging.

He had the first go with the fork until he had to pass it on. Colin had not enough breath for a word but took the sack from me and held its neck open. It was not simply that I was providing the physical energy, expressing his lust, cracking into the red carrot, sweating with youth. He was acutely conscious of everything that had to be done and was mentally hyper-active; very much in control of the operation.

It was ridiculous in a sense, remaining there for even a second after we had accomplished what we had ostensibly come for. It was pointless, of course, finishing off by digging right to the bottom, taking out the fibrous stuff and packing it round the upright pipe in the next wooden section, to have it all ready for a new season's compost.

To Colin, this plan worked with the necessary rhythm of the year. Decayed matter of weeds and peelings was rotted down but could later be extracted from the wooden frame like sections of honey. But he knew that the new owner, who would not bother to cut the grass, would never even notice the existence of the composting system.

Colin won me over. 'If you have another half-hour,' he said, 'we could finish off the thing.'

'Surely.' That came without thought. I was not speaking from either politeness or a sense of duty. Colin was carrying me. All right, so the compost was already out and awaiting collection by his son's land-rover, but we had to complete our job, make it all neat.

I set to scraping and tidying, and then stuck the fork right into the ground to let me lean against it and breathe. Colin had disappeared for a minute but returned from the car with a claw-hammer. The boot of that vehicle always did hold tools for every occasion.

I was asked to gather the short planks. Colin nailed them on, with not a pause in his hammering, and they all fitted there, sealing his boxes, the composting system. Everything was now complete, done with dignity.

It was then he opened himself, with not even a pause to return to normal breathing.

'You may think all this is plain daft,' he said, though he knew I did not. 'Of course when we came here it was to be the very final move. So we built something up. Now my son has his own place down the road, and Sarah and I have a small home arranged... It is not quite at the other end of the earth. He will be able to visit us. A more hospitable clime. You know all that. Everyone says, are you going back home? Where's that for heaven's sake? Sarah says we never go back, and she's right. If you're alive you know when it's time to move, and if you don't go you end up offering damn-all to the place.'

'Colin, you're alive,' I said. 'Nothing surer.'

'Well,' he said, 'I know what's coming and it's quite obvious that life can't just stop - oh and you can have my dinner suit with the tails, you were taken by that - yes, but neither Sarah or I are going to sit about waiting... I know I've never told you about my brother.'

This indeed came out of the blue.

'Successful man in the business world but no time for a family. Retired into a luxury apartment with nothing but furniture in it. A hell of a long day to fill. He could not bring himself up here, to the provinces, to see us, not even for a few days. No point to head for, that man, except this - he saw something that would give meaning and some purpose at least. His body could go to medical research.'

Colin started walking then and we went abreast from the garden.

'My brother died on a Friday. They did not find him until the Monday. It was too late then for him to be of any use.'

Colin's voice did not waver but I felt the tug at the roots of my shoulder as he took the fork from my hand to return it to the boot of the Austin.

THE MOVE

Armed Interventions seemed distant and I wanted to keep them like that, for the day at least. It's not often someone buys you coffee because they want to talk: they are unsettled but motivated beyond the compact headline which would incite you only to bracket-away a world-situation. People should be encouraged, to talk as well as buy me coffee, but I wasn't quite ready for global intensity, though I wanted to be involved in these views she was expounding with energy. Or maybe it was my fellow-student's rare energy itself which was so attractive.

Another day, we would talk. If my awareness would not come too late to the world.

Colin was surely not aware of interfering, right

now, but he was in mind. Yes and physically present, only a matter of a bus-ride distant. He had started the move to the town I study in, not in pursuit of me or of his own family but to establish an independent, if humble house for Sarah and himself. This town was central enough and probably small enough. There was a house that was again central in its place in a group of houses which, he and Sarah hoped, would offer safeguards to their admitted old age, but without claustrophobia. All this was explained, along with a note of the address, in a letter I had in my pocket.

Meanwhile, alongside this train of thought, she was winning. I was getting dutifully depressed. No, that is not fair to her or the issues. The cartons with fluorescent strawberry traces and wrapping papers with slogans alongside a red mess of left-over beans, were all around. The remains of many lunches. They imposed themselves as an aspect of our part of the world's consumerist reality. And I was in it, up to my sticky teeth, so was presently unable to feel the level of righteous indignation I wanted to.

I got out. Had to be honest, even if my state of mind was perilously close to 'Not Today Thank You.'

Outwith the rush-hour the bus is a fair enough method of transport. There are less fumes inside it than you meet outside when you are on a bicycle.

Sarah would not have arrived yet. Colin would be

unpacking their possessions. There would not have been a full van, but it was all good stuff. Sarah's writing desk and chair, delicate, pale and practical all at the same time, would have to find the right alcove. The lampshades she had made some time ago would go with the fine standard lamps to widen out whatever room it was.

The cigarette had long since fizzled out in his mouth. The tweed jacket was somewhere else. His working shirt had immaculate cuffs but three buttons were opened at the neck. He was sweating.

'It's good to see you. Come in, you've timed it rather well. It's a good job we don't have to depend on a younger generation. Come in for heaven's sake and mind your feet on my new carpet. I've just laid it. Quite cheap, but simple, self-coloured, practical and it will do us for as long as we need it.'

He was down to see to the fiddly jobs before Sarah arrived. She'd be there in a couple of days: not quite a hundred per cent fit, but looking forward to being settled.

'You're thatching another nest, Colin,' I offered.

'Before I offer you a cup of chronic coffee - something's going wrong with dried milk these days - you're going to give me a hand to position our possessions.'

'If you turn over the chairs like you turn the phrases, we'll do all right.'

He had already done most of the heavy lifting. This

was more a matter of artistic arrangement. We even put up the curtains. Sarah had received the measurements, done the job in tweed, and given the finished products to Colin to take down with him.

'A civilized cup of tea.' Colin altered the prescription. One tea-bag or two? They're big mugs. Let's use them while we can. The fine china will be out in a day or two.'

We sat in comfort. Colin had things organized. I was tuning-in to his crack but he must have sensed I was also struggling against a vague feeling of redundance.

'Are you hungry?' he asked. 'I'm starving. What about making dinner? You know all the shops and things around.'

I suggested a provisional menu which was approved with the rider that Colin was in charge of the sweet. He already had something half ready.

'Sarah will be down in a day or two,' he said. 'She's watching my cholestrol level, so I want to get as much as I can inside me while I have the chance.'

The move was on. I left Colin unwrapping some fine pieces of porcelain and found my own energy, enough to sprint, as soon as I was out the door.

The resultant liver and bacon casserole in a frying pan was pronounced very good, even without any oregano to sprinkle over the plum tomatoes. There

was a complaint at the scrimped amount of pota-
toes, however.

Maybe it was as well I had failed to prepare more.
Colin's sweet needed a genuine level of enthusiasm
to enact justice upon it.

As he said, there was no point in doing anything
other than halfing the baker's apple-tart. We didn't
want to have to choose between double cream and
ice-cream so they were both here. We consumed all
the tart. He allowed me to scrape the container of
cream but he had already taken his own spoon to
the remnants of ice-cream which clung to the
packet. I was happy and beyond taking note of the
brand name or contents or additives.

And he'd had an earlier idea about a small gateaux
so we couldn't let it go to waste. The bakers
seemed very good here. This town looked fairly
promising.

This central small town in a small country with an
unequal share of things. Tomorrow we would
return to moderation, Colin said it himself: bully
beef and cabbage, if I was free or could arrange to
be so.

I would be, but later in the day. I had to buy someone a cup of coffee first.

MISFITS

Five nails for the price of ten' - was the tangible and centrifugal phrase round which it all happened. It was not so much the way he told it as the way he sat while he told it. His legs were firmly crossed to show how straight-laced his brogues were but his shoulder and elbow were curiously askance, tilting with mischief over the straight back and side of his plain chair.

Before Colin reached his packet of nails he had to get the hand-me-down Hillman Imp moving. Wasn't it strange how processes reversed themselves on you? The youngest used to get what others had outgrown. Now here was the old man with what he believed was termed a neat little number. It had a fancy little steering column and the whole works had been given him by one of his sons who was moving on to more weighty things. But this particular thing refused to start.

If an aged narrator called another man old you could bet on the latter being extremely so. The fellow lived only on the other side of the reservation of Sheltered Housing but they had never spoken before until he leaned over with an air of knowing what went on under the bonnet of a motor car.

'I've written a song,' he said and then, as if antici-pating a possible question, which was not in fact the one in Colin's mind at the time, added 'And I've thought up a tune for it.'

He wanted to get if performed to a wide audience.

Had he tried the B.B.C.?

Yes, but the problem was that it wasn't the proper channel, just to go up the steps, through the swing-doors, up to the desk, open your mouth and put your head back to sing it.

Had he tried sending in a tape-recording?

That was a good idea. Was there a machine he could borrow?

So the need for the necessary implement was his reason for accosting his near-neighbour. Well, the good lady at home right then had some piece of machinery with loudspeakers that made a noise but he was pretty sure it wasn't a tape-recorder. However, there was a reputable firm that had proved very efficient in hiring out and maintaining a T.V. set for them. Why didn't he go - it was in the main thoroughfare - and ask for similar treatment for the use of a tape-recorder?

The really old man with the song, that for the time being had to be taken for granted, nodded. He would try.

The engine, which Colin believed could be termed 'souped up' sounded pretty healthy when it eventually started. It took him to the town thoroughfare without any further mishaps or meetings.

He needed five screws for a simple woodwork project which was part of the extension of his garden of window-boxes and small-area intensive lettuce production. He had achieved permission for this scheme without so far having been accused of a form of imperialism or infiltration out from his own footing on the reservation.

The shop assistant made the first objection to the whole design. This was a man dignified by a suit but without a trace of ever having worn a rough apron. He was not worth the name of Ironmonger.

'Screws, sir.' And he pointed to a stand where you could help yourself to pretty packets of ten at a grossly inflated price. This process of pre-packaged disintegration would be accepted by most customers but not by Colin. However, before he had really hit his rhetorical high-pitch another elderly man distracted the assistant.

Did they do alterations? He had been in a shop two doors away which had a sign on it: 'Baby wear and Alterations.' But they had only redirected him here.

Before the assistant could claim his right of reply the new customer lifted a substantial wool pullover to reveal an impressive and regimented array of safety pins, all down his trouser front. The problem was clear. The assistant's course of speech or action was not. He could hardly even think of another place to redirect the unwelcome traffic of old men that was breaching his peace.

You could almost expect the man who was looking for a tape-recorder to enter then and sing his song but he did not in fact re-appear.

Nor did Colin, the narrator, extend his feet nor sweep his off-hand arm and shoulder round for an emphatic ending of his tale. That would have been too neat: gathering together all his points; making a single thrust of them. It would have been too much like flourishing the five screws which he had eventually got hold of and performing a metallic match-trick with them.

He only added that Sarah was later moved to consider possible ways of providing services for such non-commercial situations. Only later did she admit the practical considerations which would have to be faced. For example, whether repairs could be conducted on the hoof as you stood your ground, or whether one would have to take one's difficulties off and hand them over the counter.

So the lost souls, or those who merely insisted on remaining a bit out of step, would continue to wander or drive or question their way around the unaccommodating streets.